THE MAN WHOSE ARMS GREW BRANCHES

TAHIR SHAH

EMILIE MAINO

THE MAN WHOSE ARMS GREW BRANCHES

A Teaching Story

TAHIR SHAH

EMILIE MAINO

MMXXIV

Secretum Mundi Publishing Ltd
124 City Road
London
EC1V 2NX
United Kingdom

www.secretum-mundi.com
info@secretum-mundi.com

First published by Secretum Mundi Publishing Ltd, 2024
A version of this story originally appeared in *Scorpion Soup* by Tahir Shah, 2013

THE MAN WHOSE ARMS GREW BRANCHES

Artwork drawn by Emilie Maino

A CIP catalogue record for this title is available from the British Library.

ISBN 978-1-915876-11-9

VERSION 31012024

Visit the author's website:
Tahirshah.com

Follow your dreams to your most distant destination,
rather than the road believed to lead there.

Uzbek saying

Teaching Stories

WHEN I WAS small, I was told stories from morning till night.

I was told stories about genies and witches and about great birds that could carry away elephants on their wings… and stories about distant kingdoms and magical lands ruled by warrior kings.

I was told stories of good and bad… stories of hope and others of despair.

I was even told stories about stories.

And all the while, I listened, amazed.

The more I listened, the more my mind worked… and the more I came to understand that these stories had a power about them, a secret lifeblood all of their own.

They were magical instruments, machineries that could alter states of mind and change the way we think.

But most importantly of all, stories can teach us, without us realizing that they are doing so at all.

Part of the default programming of man, stories are within us all.

Born into us, they make us who we are – they make us human.

Since earliest childhood, I have feasted on stories as a way of learning about the world, and learning about myself. They have been my dictionary and my encyclopaedia, my classroom, my guide, and my very best friend.

To descend down through the layers of stories is to be reborn, into a dominion of fantasy – one touched by real magic.

Pre-eminent within the great treasuries of tales, it is teaching stories like this one that have shown me the path to follow beyond the next horizon, and have made me the man I am.

Tahir Shah

Once upon a time, in a land far from here, a traveller named Youssef was making his way through a forest when he became disorientated and lost.

When night fell, he bedded down on a patch of dry leaves beneath a magnificent oak tree and did his best to drift into sleep.

Little did he know, however,
that the oak under which he was
lying had not always been a tree.

As Youssef tossed and turned in the leaves,
he heard a voice:
'Hello, young adventurer, I am so pleased
that I may be of service to you.'

Fearful and startled, Youssef sat upright.
'Who's there?!'

The tree spoke again,
a little louder than before:
'It's me, the oak under whose branches you are
taking shelter, and in whose leaves you are
nestling for the night.'

Assuming it to be the trickery of a jinn,
the traveller recited a prayer, one known
to ward away the most malevolent evil.

Branches swaying, the tree spoke a third time:
'My name is such-and-such, and although
you may not believe it from my current
appearance, I was once a man just like you.'

Polite by nature, even to trees,
Youssef didn't want to cause offence.

‘Please believe me when I say that I wish you well,’ he answered, ‘but unless there is some sinister force at work, I don’t understand how a man could have become an oak tree.’

Swaying more forcefully than before,
the tree asked for permission to tell his story.
'Nothing would interest me more,'
said the traveller.

And so, clearing his throat,
the tree told his tale:

'I used to run through the fields and the forests,' he said. 'And I'd play with my brothers and sisters in the long summer days. The world was perfect then, and we used to be thankful for the warmth on our faces and for the soft ground beneath our feet.

‘But most of all, we were thankful for the trees.

‘We would climb them, carve our names on their trunks, swing from them and lie in their branches, bragging of all the adventures we would have in the years ahead.

'One summer evening, I climbed to the very top of a soaring beech tree and looked out over the forest. The view was astonishing – a carpet of green, an immensity that could never be dominated, even by man.

‘Or so I thought.

‘Years passed and, before I knew it, I was no longer a child but an adult with a wife and children of my own. However hard I worked in the town, I never had enough money to make ends meet.

‘My wife used to scold me, declaring that I didn’t strive hard enough in the market. My problem was that there just wasn’t enough work.

‘Then, one day, I overheard a wealthy man telling a stallkeeper that he had made a fortune in the timber business. He had been given the right to chop down trees in a land to the west of our own.

‘My ears pricked up, because the thought of being in the countryside and gaining real wealth was extremely interesting.

'The next thing I knew,
I had become a woodcutter.

‘I bought the very best axe I could afford and chopped down trees from morning until night. I was strong and athletic, and found that I could do the job far better than anyone else.

‘Within a few months, I had paid my debts and had cleared a huge swathe of forest. And within a couple of years, I was rich, and my wife was dressed in fine satins and silks.

‘But, as is the way of women,
she wanted more.

‘And more, and more.

‘So I kept chopping, cutting down all the trees I found in my path – great big trees and tiny saplings.

‘Nothing escaped my blade.

'One morning, deep in the forest where I was camping, I was unsheathing my axe when a little turquoise bird flew down and perched on my shoulder.

"'"Please stop chopping down our forest," said the bird in my ear. "All the birds and the other animals are suffering because of you. If you don't stop, the forest will take revenge."

‘Swishing the little creature away, I got down to my work and, that day alone, I hacked down thirty trees.

'Time slipped by, and I made more and more money – so much so that I hired a team of woodcutters and got them to work for me.

‘We bought better and better axes and each week I became more wealthy. But, needless to say, my wife found ways to spend all the money I earned.

‘Then, one day, I woke up with a pain in my hand. I assumed it was from years of chopping wood, and so I rested.

‘A few days passed, and a pain began bothering my other hand. A week on, and something very strange indeed happened.

‘A little green shoot sprouted from my elbow.

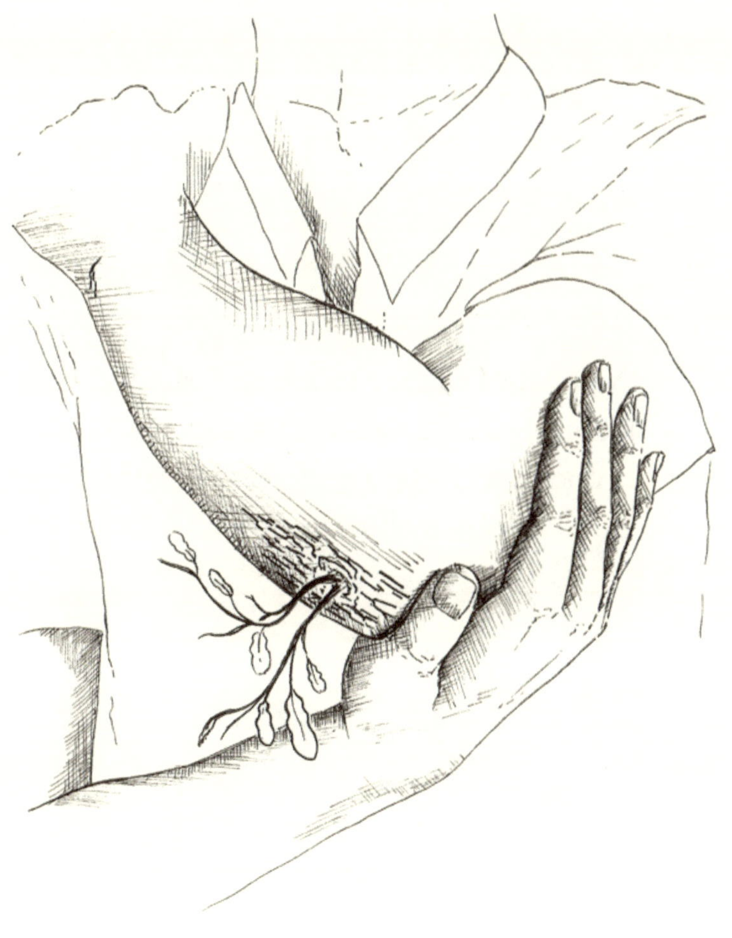

‘Naturally, I was very alarmed. I showed it to my wife. Screaming, she sent me to a doctor and left to visit her mother in the neighbouring town.

‘The doctor prescribed a tonic and told me to get rest. So I took to my bed for a week, drinking the tonic morning and night.

'As I lay there under the blanket,
the shoot continued to grow.

'It grew and it grew, and it grew and it grew, until it was more of a branch than a simple shoot.

'At the same time, another shoot sprouted on my other elbow, and on both my hands. Before I knew it, there were shoots peeping out from each finger, and from my ears as well.

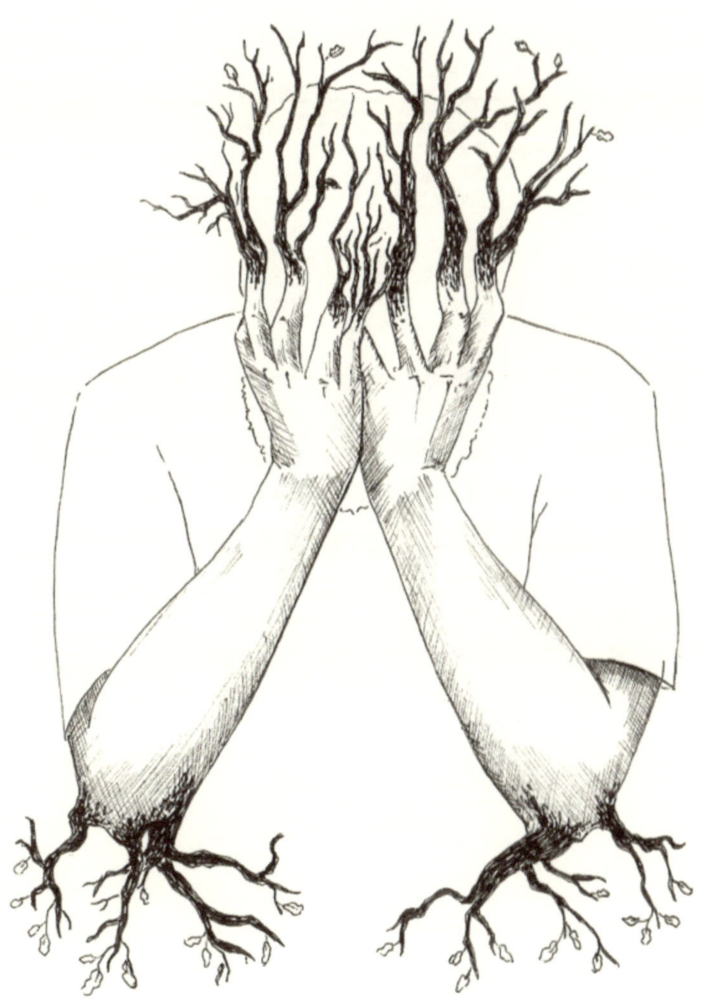

‘I was both terrified and ashamed. No one else
I knew had foliage growing from their body.

'After three weeks, my wife returned from her mother's home. By this time, my entire frame was covered in greenery.

‘Vines were growing out of my nostrils
and my face was rough and grey like
the trunk of a tree.

‘And that is what I was becoming
– an oak tree.

'My wife ordered me to leave the house at once. She said I was bewitched, that I had brought dishonour to our home.

'Confused and humiliated, I set off
– to get away from people.

'Whenever anyone saw me, they taunted me, calling me an oddity and a cursed mutant.

‘And then, one day, I reached the forest
where we now find ourselves.

'By that time I had lost the use of my arms, with branches in their place. My torso was more like a tree's trunk than a human body and, with each moment, I felt my legs stiffen a little more.

'As for my toes, they had become roots
– roots searching for soft ground in which
to plant themselves.

'I knew deep down in my sap why this change in circumstances had come. It was of course retribution from the forest for having felled so many fine trees with my axe.'

The oak tree paused for a moment as a light breeze rippled through his leaves.

He seemed to sigh.

'All this happened centuries ago,' he said. 'I suppose I should be thankful because I have outlived all the people I once knew.'

The oak sighed again.

‘I wish I could pass on a message urgently to the humans,’ he said, ‘to teach them to change the path they have begun to tread.’

Youssef shrugged.

'What path ought they to follow, then?'

‘One which allows them to think of the whole rather than merely of oneself… and to spare a thought for the generations that will come.’

Moved by the tree's story and his advice, the traveller touched a hand to the oak's great trunk.

‘I shall devote what time I have left to making this knowledge available to all men,’ he said.

The oak tree's leaves rustled with pleasure.
'Would you tell me the message?' he asked.

Next morning, Youssef thanked the tree for his shelter, and the tree lowered a twig for him to shake.

Just as the traveller turned to go,
the tree gave a little snort.
'I have been thinking,' he said humbly, 'and
I want to help you spread the message I passed
on to you last night.'

Youssef frowned.

'What do you mean?' he said. 'I don't want to appear discourteous, but you are a tree. I am grateful to you for providing the message, but I don't grasp how you can help me now pass it on.'

Standing even taller and prouder than before, the oak tree spoke:

'From my branches you can make paper,' he said, 'and from my twigs you can fashion a nib. From the oak apples in my high branches you can make ink.

‘And,’ he said,
his voice quivering ever so slightly, ‘when
you are done creating a book from me, you
can make a beautiful casket from my torso
in which to keep that book.’

Youssef took in the mighty oak's wide trunk,
its branches, its twigs, leaves, and shoots.
'Dear oak, I could not betray your kindness,'
he said.

The oak tree replied:
'Even after I have betrayed the forest, among which I have now lived for an eternity? Cut me down, and I shall begin life in a new form.'

And so, a tear in his eye,
Youssef felled the tree.

He made paper from its twigs, and ink from the oak apples, and sewed the binding with twine made from its roots.

Once he had created a huge tome standing as at least tall as a man, he fashioned a magnificent chest to contain it, delicately carved and scented with the fragrance of the forest.

And on the front of the chest,
he inscribed the following words:

My form may have changed,
but I contain the wisdom required by all men.

My form may
have changed,
but I contain the
wisdom required
by all men.

The chest was heaved onto a grand cart and transported to the National Library, where it was presented as a gift to all the people of the land.

But, as there was no place in the main hall large enough to display the enormous box and the book it contained, it was dragged down into the cellars beneath the library.

A few days after its arrival, the kingdom was overthrown by an invading army.

Much of the population were slaughtered,
including Youssef.

All the libraries were destroyed by fire,
and anyone found owning a book was
burned at the stake.

The only book that survived was the one made from the ancient oak tree, because it was down in the cellars, protected by the colossal wooden box.

The invading despot gave the order for the farmland of the vanquished country to be tilled with salt. So ruthless was his new regime that the people fled to other kingdoms, their lands unfit to be ploughed, their capital destroyed.

Eventually, and with all the people gone,
nature reclaimed the ruins of the city.

Where the capital had once stood,
a forest grew, giant oaks forming an
almost impenetrable barricade against
the outside world.

A century passed.

And another.

Then, one summer afternoon, a hunter strayed into the forest on the trail of gazelle when he became disorientated and lost.

Night fell quickly, forcing him to bed down on a rock, itself covered in moss.

Awaking the next morning, the hunter realized that he had sought shelter in what appeared to be the ruins of an ancient building.

Surveying the area, he descended into what were once the cellars, where he found the enormous carved wooden chest, all covered in creepers and vines.

Carefully, he cut away the lianas. And with all his strength, he pushed back the lid.

Inside, perfectly protected,
was the colossal book.

A book that revealed to the hunter
the wisdom he had waited for his entire life.

But, more importantly, wisdom that the world was now ready to receive.

Finis

About the Author

Descended from a long line of storytellers, writers, and savants, Tahir Shah is one of the most prolific authors of his generation. He has published more than sixty books in numerous genres, including travel, fiction, and fantasy, as well as tales for children.

Raised in the tradition of Eastern 'teaching stories', Shah is passionate about stories and storytelling. He regards the ability to learn from folklore as being in us all, what he calls a 'default setting of humankind'. As well as having written scores of books, Shah has made documentaries for National Geographic TV and The History Channel. He is the founder and CEO of the charity, The Scheherazade Foundation.

Books By Tahir Shah

The Writer's Craft

The Reason to Write

Workbook: Comprehensive, Volume I & II

Workbook: Fantasy, Volume I & II

Workbook: Fiction, Volume I & II

Workbook: Historical Fiction, Volume I & II

Workbook: Teaching Stories, Volume I & II

Workbook: Travel, Volume I & II

Novels

Jinn Hunter: Book One – The Prism

Jinn Hunter: Book Two – The Jinnslayer

Jinn Hunter: Book Three – The Perplexity

Hannibal Fogg and the Supreme Secret of Man

Casablanca Blues

Eye Spy

Godman

Paris Syndrome

Timbuctoo

Midas

Zigzagzone

Nasrudin

Travels With Nasrudin

The Misadventures of the Mystifying Nasrudin

The Peregrinations of the Perplexing Nasrudin

The Voyages and Vicissitudes of Nasrudin

Nasrudin in the Land of Fools

Travel

Trail of Feathers

Travels With Myself

Beyond the Devil's Teeth

In Search of King Solomon's Mines

House of the Tiger King

In Arabian Nights

The Caliph's House

Sorcerer's Apprentice

Journey Through Namibia

Teaching Stories

The Arabian Nights Adventures

Scorpion Soup

Tales Told to a Melon

The Afghan Notebook

Daydreams of an Octopus & Other Stories

The Caravanserai Stories

Ghoul Brothers

Hourglass

Imaginist

Jinn's Treasure

Jinnlore

Mellified Man

Skeleton Island

Wellspring

When the Sun Forgot to Rise

Outrunning the Reaper

The Cap of Invisibility

On Backgammon Time

The Wondrous Seed

The Paradise Tree
Mouse House
The Hoopoe's Flight
The Old Wind
A Treasury of Tales
The Tale of Double Six
The Forgotten Game
King of the Jinns
The Destiny Ring
Changing the World
Cat, Mouse
Frogland
Mittle-Mittle
Capilongo
The Princess of Zilzilam
The Singing Serpents
The Tale of the Rusty Nail
The Unicorn's Tear
The Clockmaker Who Travelled Through Time
The Fish's Dream
The Man Whose Arms Grew Branches
The Most Foolish of Men
The Shop That Sold Truth
Qwerty
Renaissance
The Man With the Tiger's Head
The Kingdom of Blink
The Wisdom of Celestine
Dream Soup
The Skeleton Factory
An Unexpected Gift

The Problem Exchange
The Pharaoh Code
The Monkey Puzzle Club
Liquid Time
Cat Dog, Dog Cat
Princess Pickle's Laugh

Anthologies

The Anthologies: Africa
The Anthologies: Ceremony
The Anthologies: Childhood
The Anthologies: City
The Anthologies: Danger
The Anthologies: East
The Anthologies: Expedition
The Anthologies: Frontier
The Anthologies: Hinterland
The Anthologies: India
The Anthologies: Jinns
The Anthologies: Jungle
The Anthologies: Magic
The Anthologies: Morocco
The Anthologies: Nasrudin
The Anthologies: People
The Anthologies: Quest
The Anthologies: South
The Anthologies: Taboo
The Anthologies: Teaching Stories
The Clockmaker's Box
The Tahir Shah Fiction Reader
The Tahir Shah Travel Reader

Research

Cultural Research

The Middle East Bedside Book

Three Essays

Edited by

Congress With a Crocodile

A Son of a Son, Volume I

A Son of a Son, Volume II

Screenplays

Casablanca Blues: The Screenplay

Timbuctoo: The Screenplay

A REQUEST

If you enjoyed this book, please review it on your favourite online retailer or review website.

Reviews are an author's best friend.

To stay in touch with Tahir Shah, and to hear about his upcoming releases before anyone else, please sign up for his mailing list:

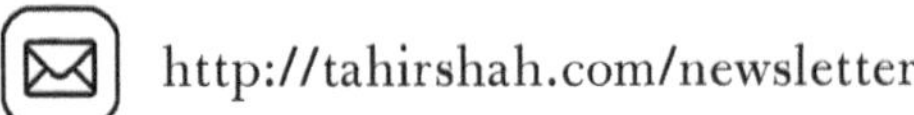
http://tahirshah.com/newsletter

And to follow him on social media, please go to any of the following links:

http://www.twitter.com/humanstew

@tahirshah999

http://www.facebook.com/TahirShahAuthor

http://www.youtube.com/user/tahirshah999

http://www.pinterest.com/tahirshah

https://www.goodreads.com/tahirshahauthor

http://www.tahirshah.com

www.ingramcontent.com/pod-product-compliance
Lightning Source LLC
Chambersburg PA
CBHW030522310726
48979CB00010B/1766/J

* 9 7 8 1 9 1 5 8 7 6 1 1 9 *